THOMAS & FRIENDS™

Thomas Scares the Crows!

D0794652

The farmers of Sodor were planting corn seeds. When Thomas pulled up at Farmer McColl's farm, he heard a loud noise.

Squawk! Squawk! Squawk!

There were crows **everywhere!**

Farmer McColl was **not** happy. The crows were eating all of his seeds!

"Shoo!" Farmer McColl shouted at the birds. "My scarecrow needs fixing. These crows are ruining my corn field!"

An idea flew into Thomas' funnel. He could scare the crows away by making lots of noise!

Toot! Toot! Toot!

Sure enough, the crows flapped away. But a few minutes later, they all came back.

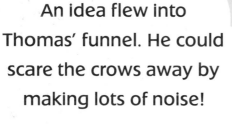

"I'll keep these birds away until you fix your scarecrow," Thomas told Farmer McColl.

But two of the crows ignored Thomas' toots and hoots.

So Thomas had another idea. He would chase those birds far away from the field!

Thomas **puffed** his pistons and lurched towards the birds. The crows squawked and flew off down the track.

"I'm right behind you!" huffed Thomas, steaming after the birds.

The crows flew faster. Thomas' boiler **bubbled**. "I must chase them away!"

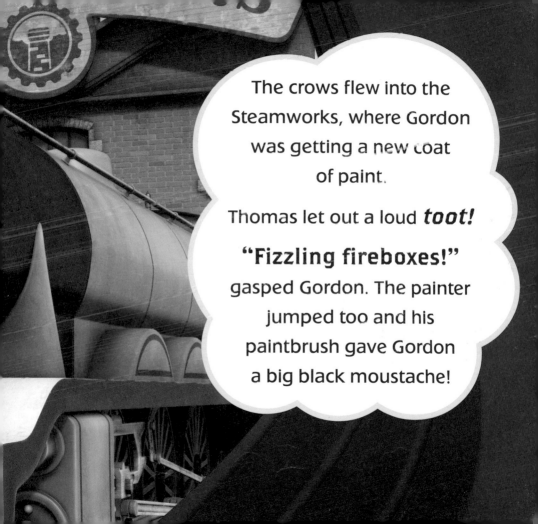

The crows flew into the Steamworks, where Gordon was getting a new coat of paint.

Thomas let out a loud *toot!*

"Fizzling fireboxes!" gasped Gordon. The painter jumped too and his paintbrush gave Gordon a big black moustache!

"Sorry, Gordon!" giggled Thomas. "Can't stop …"

The crows flew back up into the sky. They were ready for another chase!

Thomas **huffed** and **puffed** and *tooted* as loud as he could. Chasing crows away was hard work!

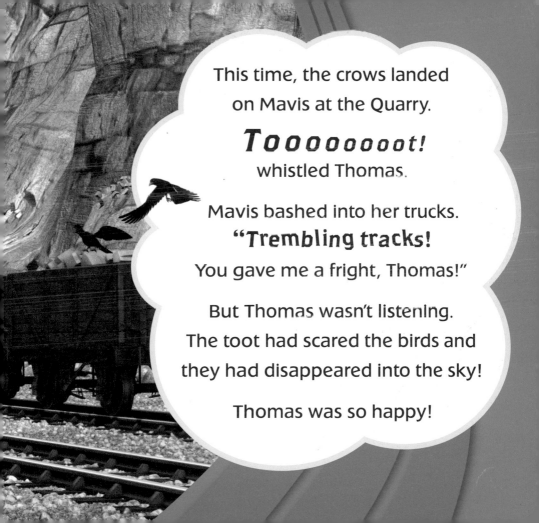

This time, the crows landed
on Mavis at the Quarry.

Tooooooot!
whistled Thomas.

Mavis bashed into her trucks.
"Trembling tracks!
You gave me a fright, Thomas!"

But Thomas wasn't listening.
The toot had scared the birds and
they had disappeared into the sky!

Thomas was so happy!

But Farmer McColl was not so happy. When Thomas arrived at the farm, the crows were back already. And they'd brought even more of their friends with them too!

"What am I going to do?" sighed Farmer McColl. "The scarecrow won't be ready until the morning."

Thomas felt terrible. If only he had stayed at the field, as he'd promised. "I'll watch your field tonight, Famer McColl. I won't move a piston!"

This time, Thomas kept to his word. He hooted and tooted all night long.

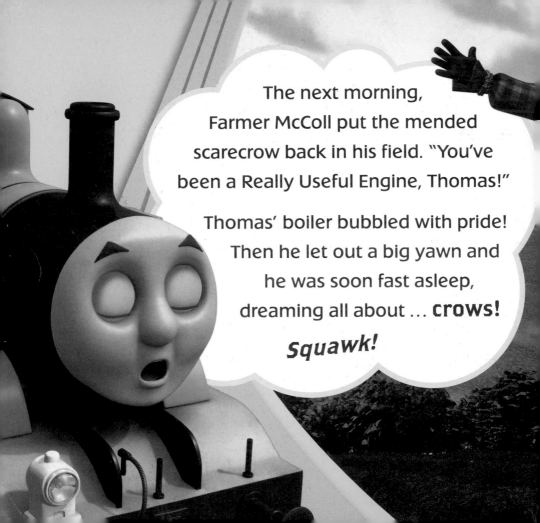

The next morning, Farmer McColl put the mended scarecrow back in his field. "You've been a Really Useful Engine, Thomas!"

Thomas' boiler bubbled with pride! Then he let out a big yawn and he was soon fast asleep, dreaming all about ... **crows!**

Squawk!

The End